This edition published by Parragon in 2013
Parragon
Chartist House
15–17 Trim Street
Bath BA1 1HA, UK
www.parragon.com

ISBN 978-1-4723-1081-1

Printed in China

# The Three Billy Goats Gruff

Retold by Ronne Randall

Illustrated by Gavin Scott

PaRragon

Bath · New York · Singapore · Hong Kong · Cologne · Delhi
Melbourne · Amsterdam · Johannesburg · Shenzhen

Once upon a time, there were three Billy Goats Gruff who lived on a hillside near a river.

There was Little Billy Goat Gruff, Middle Billy Goat Gruff, and Great Big Billy Goat Gruff.

They ate the grass on the hillside, and grew fatter and fatter.

One day, the three Billy Goats Gruff looked around and saw that they had eaten all the grass on the hillside!

"What shall we do now?" Little Billy Goat Gruff asked his brothers. "If we don't find more grass, we will waste away!"

"There is plenty of **yummy, green grass** over there," said Middle Billy Goat Gruff, looking at a meadow on the other side of the river.

"Yes," said his big brother, Great Big Billy Goat Gruff. "All we have to do is cross the wooden bridge, and we can eat to our hearts' content!"

But the bridge was guarded by a horrible, ugly troll.

He was **green**, with a **great big head** and a **bright red nose**.

There were **warts on his skin** and **hairs on his chin**, and his terrible teeth were **long and pointy and yellow**.

And he was very SMELLY!

"Which one of us will be brave enough to cross that bridge?" Great Big Billy Goat Gruff asked his brothers.

The three Billy Goats Gruff all looked at each other.

At last, Little Billy Goat Gruff piped up,
"I will cross the bridge!"

And off he went, down the hillside.

Trip, trap, trip, trap,

he went over the wooden bridge.

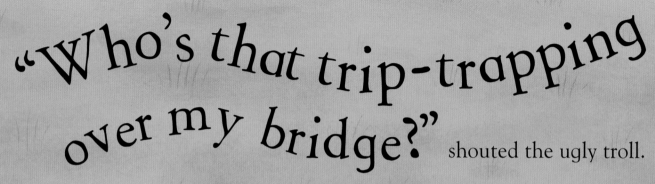

"Who's that trip-trapping over my bridge?" shouted the ugly troll.

"It is I, Little Billy Goat Gruff," the goat replied, trying not to breathe in the troll's horrible smell. "I'm just going over to the meadow to eat the green grass."

"No, you're not!" growled the troll.
"I'm going to eat YOU first!" And he
climbed up onto the little wooden bridge.

Little Billy Goat Gruff was very frightened, but he knew what to say.

"I don't think I would make a very good meal for you. Can't you see how little I am? You should wait for my brother, Middle Billy Goat Gruff. He is much **bigger** and **fatter** than me!"

The troll thought about it. **"All right,"** he said. **"You may cross the bridge."**

So Little Billy Goat Gruff went **trip, trap, trip, trap** across the wooden bridge and skipped into the meadow.

As soon as he saw that Little Billy Goat Gruff was safe, Great Big Billy Goat Gruff said to his younger brother, "It's your turn now."

So Middle Billy Goat Gruff trotted down the hillside.

Trip, trap, trip, trap,

he went over the wooden bridge.

When he was halfway across, the smelly troll shouted,

# "Who's that trip-trapping over my bridge?"

"It is I, Middle Billy Goat Gruff," said the goat. "I am just going over the bridge to eat the green grass with my brother on the other side."

"Oh no, you're not," shouted the troll. "I'm going to eat YOU first!" And he climbed right up onto the little wooden bridge.

Middle Billy Goat Gruff was very frightened, but he didn't let the troll see that.

"There's not much meat on my bones," he said. "You should wait for my brother, Great Big Billy Goat Gruff. He is the biggest and fattest of us all, and he would make a much tastier meal for you."

"All right," said the troll. "You may cross the bridge."

So Middle Billy Goat Gruff went

# trip, trap, trip, trap

over the wooden bridge
to join his brother in the
meadow on the other side.

At last, it was Great Big Billy Goat Gruff's turn to cross the bridge.

Trip, trap, trip, trap

went his hooves on the wooden bridge.

"Who's that trip-trapping over my bridge?" bellowed the troll.

"It is I, Great Big Billy Goat Gruff.
I am going to join my brothers to eat
the green grass in the meadow."

"Oh no, you're not!"
thundered the troll.

"You are the biggest,
fattest Billy Goat
Gruff, and I'm going
to eat YOU!"

And the smelly troll clambered up
onto the bridge.

Great Big Billy Goat Gruff was not afraid of the horrible, ugly troll. But the troll was certainly afraid when he saw Great Big Billy Goat Gruff! He tried to run away, but before he could, Great Big Billy Goat Gruff lowered his head, stamped his hooves and, with his great big billy goat horns, he butted the troll right into the river!

The troll went under the water with a great big

SPLASH

and was never, ever seen again.

Then Great Big Billy Goat Gruff went

trip, trap, trip, trap

over the wooden bridge to join his brothers in the meadow.

All three of them ate yummy, green grass, and they grew **bigger** and **fatter**, and happier every day!

# The End